Schoolmaster Whackwell's Wonderful Sons

Other books translated from the German
by *Doris Orgel* and illustrated by *Maurice Sendak:*

DWARF LONG-NOSE
by Wilhelm Hauff

THE TALE OF GOCKEL, HINKEL & GACKELIAH
by Clemens Brentano

A FAIRY TALE BY

CLEMENS BRENTANO

Schoolmaster Whackwell's Wonderful Sons

RETOLD BY DORIS ORGEL

ILLUSTRATED BY MAURICE SENDAK

RANDOM HOUSE  NEW YORK

 Published in New York by Random House, Inc., and simultaneously in Toronto, Canada, by Random House of Canada, Limited.

Library of Congress Catalog Card Number: 62-9002

Manufactured in the United States of America by Random House, Inc.

Design by Peter Oldenburg and Sophie Adler

for Paul

for Laura

for Jeremy

PREFACE

Clemens Brentano was born in 1778, in Ehrenbreitstein on the Rhine; he died in 1842, in the little town of Aschaffenburg. He was a poet, a story teller, and a writer of very serious books for grown-ups. Those are some facts which German children are taught about Brentano in their schools.

There is another fact, though, which they would find more remarkable and interesting, if only they were taught it: While he was still a boy, this Clemens Brentano was an *emperor*. The name of his empire was Vaduz (he pronounced it Vadoots—you can say it anyway you like), and it was a little land full of all the strangest secrets and wonders of the world. Where was it? No one knows for sure, because its emperor carefully kept that a secret. But we do know where its archives and treasures were kept—in the emperor's grandmother's attic! Up there, there were boxes of old Christmas decorations, a collection of exquisite miniature wax figures, his grandmother's bridal gown, and other fineries "with ruffles and puffs of silks and laces...that were like the mountains and valleys of a fairyland," and a magic garden where the flowers, made of silk and wire, never faded.

It was to this garden that the young emperor fled sometimes, to read or dream or do nothing at all, when his parents wanted him to go elsewhere with them, to less wonderful places. (No, this is no secret. The emperor himself confessed it to his grandmother, and so it is all right that you should know.) I think it was up there, in the magic garden of the treasure chamber of Vaduz, that stories like the one you are about to read were born.

Doris Orgel

ONCE UPON A TIME, there was a man called Whackwell, and he had five sons. The first one was called Gripsgrabs, the second, Splishsplosh, the third, Piffpaff, the fourth, Pinkiepank, and the fifth was called Tiraling.

Schoolmaster Whackwell loved his sons dearly and longed to have them learn an honest trade. But he lived in great want, for the village had burned down, and the school too, and the farmers too, and the schoolboys too; only he and his five sons remained.

Therefore he sat himself down on a stone in the middle of the burned-out village, and his five sons stood about him, and he spoke to them: "My sons, I have suddenly become a poor man, and much as I would like to give you a proper education, I lack the means; for I cannot say learned things on an empty stomach, and besides, all my ABC books were burned up in the school. Therefore I must send you out into the world, to fend for yourselves. As for me, I shall build a hut from the wood that is lying about here. You will return in a year's time, and tell me what you have learned. Meanwhile, may each of you follow his calling, and so farewell!"

Then the sons said: "We shall do faithfully what you ask of us. But Father, since you tell us to follow our calling, pray tell us, what may our calling be?"

The schoolmaster thought a while, and said: "Why, your calling is that which calls you."

Then the sons asked again: "But Father, what *is* it that calls us?"

And the schoolmaster said: "Your name calls you."

Then the sons said: "You, Father, your name is Whackwell . . . what is your calling?"

This made the father very impatient, and he said: "A fool can ask more questions than ten learned men

can answer. Yes, my name is Whackwell, and my calling is Whackwell . . . that is, to whack well such silly fools as you!" He took his cane and would have whacked them, but they ran away as fast as they could.

When evening came, they lay down in a forest, and

talked about what their callings might be. Suddenly they heard some passers-by conversing. One passer-by said to the other: "Was not that a steep castle wall?" And the other replied: "Yes, but we climbed it as we always do, gripping our daggers in our hands. Then we entered the castle, grabbed the silverware, and so it went merrily, gripsgrabs!"

No sooner did Gripsgrabs hear his name spoken, than he jumped up and said to his brothers: "Gripsgrabs is my name, it calls me! That same gripsgrabs shall my calling be, for which God in Heaven created me. In a year we shall meet again at our father's hut. Until then, farewell." And he hurried after the people who had spoken of gripsgrabs.

Toward morning, the youngest brother, Tiraling, heard the birds in the forest trill and go tiraling. "Good-bye, dear brothers," said he. "Tiraling is my name, it calls me! That same tiraling shall my calling be, for which God in Heaven created me." With that he took his leave of them, and ran deeper into the forest.

Soon the three remaining brothers came to a meadow where many people stood shooting arrows at a target, and every arrow went: *piffpaff!* Then Piffpaff said: "Piffpaff is my name, it calls me! That same piffpaff shall my calling be, for which God in Heaven created me." He took his leave of the other two, and went to the marksmen.

The two who were left went through the town, when suddenly they heard *pinkiepank*, *pinkiepank*, and looked around. There stood an apothecary banging in his mortar, *pinkiepank*, *pinkiepank*. Then brother Pinkiepank took leave of the last, saying: "Pinkiepank is my name, it calls me! That same pinkiepank shall my calling be, for which God in Heaven created me." And he went to the apothecary.

Splishsplosh, all alone now, came to a river he wanted to cross. So he called out to the boatmen on the other side: "Come and get me!" They climbed into their rowboat and came for him, their oars going *splishsplosh* all the time. Merrily he jumped in with them, saying: "Splishsplosh is my name, it calls me! That same splishsplosh shall my calling be, for which God in Heaven created me." And he remained with the boatmen.

BY THE TIME the year had gone by, Schoolmaster Whackwell had rebuilt his hut in the shade of a big tree. On the day his sons were to return from the wide world, he cooked some potatoes and put them in a bowl on the table. Then there was a knocking at the door, and four of his sons came in, quite proper and well dressed. Only Tiraling was missing.

Whackwell embraced all four, and asked where Tiraling might be. They said: "He stands outside the door and is ashamed, because he looks so ugly."

The father went outside and saw Tiraling standing under the tree, staring up at the sky. He looked unkempt and ragged, his face was brown as a berry, and he spoke not a word, making only some very odd whistling and warbling sounds. "Let the poor fellow be," said Whackwell. "He has gone mad. Perhaps he will come in later. Now sit down and eat." So they sat down at the table, and while they were eating, the father asked the eldest son: "Gripsgrabs, what have you learned in the world?"

The eldest son replied:

"Gripsgrabs is my name,
It called me! That same
Gripsgrabs must my calling be,
For which God in Heaven created me.

"Father, I have learned gripsgrabs, and am such a clever thief that I can steal anything, even if it lies locked under a hundred locks! Also, with the help of my two daggers, I can climb the steepest tower as easily as going up a ladder!"

"That is a godless art!" cried the father. "I beg of you, for Heaven's sake, turn to something else, or you will have to learn to climb the gallows, but without your two daggers! And what have *you* learned?" he asked, turning to the second son, who replied:

"Piffpaff is my name,
It called me! That same
Piffpaff must my calling be,
For which God in Heaven created me.

"Father, I went with the marksmen and have learned to shoot so well that I can shoot a worm from the beak of a swallow in flight!"

"That is a better skill," said the father. "God bless you for it." Then he asked the third son: "What have you learned?" And the third son replied:

"Pinkiepank is my name,
It called me! That same
Pinkiepank must my calling be,
For which God in Heaven created me.

"I heard the apothecary banging, *pinkiepank*, in his mortar, and became an apothecary. Now I know a little herb, Arise, that heals all wounds and cures all ills."

"The Lord be praised," said the father, "for you can help us all, and if your little herb, Arise, proves true, then there will be an arising for us which should make us as rich as any folk on earth. But tell me, what have *you* learned?" he asked the fourth son, who replied:

"Splishsplosh is my name,
It called me! That same
Splishsplosh must my calling be,
For which God in Heaven created me.'

"Father, I heard the boatmen's oars go *splishsplosh* in the water, so I became a boatman, and have a little boat which can go as fast as a swallow that darts over the water."

"Excellent," said the schoolmaster. "You have learned a good, honest skill! One day you must take us all out to sea, and who knows what wonderful things we shall find!"

THEN SCHOOLMASTER WHACKWELL opened the door and called: "Tiraling! Come in and tell us what you have learned in the world. I do believe you have taken to bear skinning, because you look so wild and shaggy."

But the good Tiraling said nothing. Instead, he stared up at the sky, and again he whistled and warbled, sounding more like a bird than a man. This made Whackwell very angry. "Let us finish eating," he said to his other sons, "and leave your brother to make his silly bird noises out there."

Tiraling came in at last. "Fie, fie!" cried Schoolmaster Whackwell. "Just look at you! You are as black as the soil, and one could hoe and sow on you! Now there is nothing left to eat. Why did you not come when I called you?"

"Because I was waiting for a messenger, who has not yet arrived," Tiraling replied. "Don't worry about my dinner, Father. I will find something good to eat." Before they could ask what message he awaited, or what he would find to eat, Tiraling dashed out again. Soon he returned, holding a big head of cabbage which he began to eat as if it were an apple.

His father and brothers had to laugh at the sight of him eating a raw cabbage. "You may laugh," said Tiraling, "but there is much to learn in the wide world about different ways and customs." Then, all of a sudden, he saw a fat fly, and snapped his jaws together . . . *snap!* "Delicious," said he. "It was a Spanish one . . . just the thing to warm up my stomach and help me digest the cabbage! But tell me, Father, don't you have any spiders here?"

"Shame on you!" said the schoolmaster. "Would you eat spiders, too?"

"Father, you don't know how good they are!" Tiraling replied. "You have never tried them. If the Apostle John could eat grasshoppers in the desert, why should I be so proud as to scorn spiders?"

Whackwell said no more about spiders, but asked again what Tiraling had learned in the world. "Tell me, my son," he said. "I do believe it is the hermit's trade."

"Yes, Father," Tiraling answered. "But that is not all. I have learned much more. You said we should follow our calling, and when we asked what that is, you said: 'Whatever calls you, that is your calling.' Well, as I was walking through the wood and heard a thousand birds go tiraling, I thought to myself:

> Tiraling is my name,
> It calls me! That same
> Tiraling must my calling be,
> For which God in Heaven created me.

"So I followed the song of the birds farther and farther, all the way into the deep, deep wood. The darker and denser the wood, the louder it called me, and the stronger my calling became. At last I reached a very lonely, silent place, where there was a high rock and a lovely stream and a most pleasant bit of lawn surrounded by the most beautiful oak trees, beeches, birches, lindens, pines and hemlocks. The sun was setting; it was time to rest. I sat leaning against an oak and ate the piece of bread that was left from what you gave us to take along.

"As I was sitting there, I saw an astounding number of birds come flying in swarms from all directions, and take possession of the trees. They began such a tiraling that one might have thought each little leaf on every tree were starting in to sing. But all at once came a loud whistling, and then they were all suddenly still, as if a sharp knife had cut their singing away from their beaks. It reminded me of school, Father dear, when you used to pound the table with your cane and call out, 'Silence!' Soon all the birds joined in the whistling, not any which-way, but all to

the same beat, in the melody of an evening song. At first I was struck dumb by such amazing unison; then I, too, began to whistle. When the birds had finished the last verse, they were silent again . . . one might have thought they were praying. After that, they began a great twittering, as if they were wishing one another a good night, whereupon they parted and flew to their various nests.

"The birds' wondrous music made me very thoughtful. I resolved to stay with them and learn to understand their singing. But I did not wish to spend the night on the ground, for, after all, this was a wild place, and I heard rustling in the bushes, as if all sorts of animals were roaming about. So I climbed a tree, and was glad I had, for I soon saw some large animal come down from another tree nearby. Whatever it was, it crept on all fours to the stream and drank. Then a boar came along—I recognized it by its grunts—and started to wallow in the water. This annoyed the other animal, and it grunted too, just as if it were scolding

the boar for muddying the stream. But the boar would not stop until the other animal gave it a powerful slap, whereupon, with great wailing, the boar ran away into the wood.

"I was more than a little frightened when the strange animal came to my tree and began to climb it. I trembled all over, thinking it would surely slap me, too. In terror, I climbed higher up into the tree. The animal must have heard me move about. It barked like a dog, and came creeping up close behind me. It seemed to know the branches of the tree better than I, for it made not a single false move, while I kept coming to thinner and thinner branches. All of a sudden, to add to my troubles, I saw a pair of fiery eyes—a screech owl was beating its wings at me—and all too close behind me was the big, barking animal. I wondered how to save myself, when suddenly the branch broke beneath me and . . . plop! I fell, with a great crackling of twigs, from branch to branch down to the ground.

"Luckily I was not hurt, but I dared not make the slightest move or utter a sound, for fear the dreadful beast would come and find me where I lay. It did not come. It merely barked a while, and then it was still.

"Soon I heard a most horrible snoring, as loud as if someone were sawing wood. 'Oh,' thought I, 'what a hideous maw the beast must have, to snore so!' Then the moon rose over the wood and poured its glitter through the trees. Surely its light would reveal what sort of creature I had encountered . . . one that could slap a boar and grunt, and climb trees, and bark like a dog! I peered up at the tree from which I had fallen, and saw the beast's form on a branch where it lay snoring. It was covered all over with long, thick hair, so that I could still not make out what it was. While I was looking up, I had another fright: The beast stretched itself and yawned most terribly... *uah*,

uah...and sneezed so mightily that the acorns came rushing down on my nose like a hailstorm. But then, imagine my amazement when all of a sudden I heard it sing the following lovely song with a loud, clear voice:

'Come, nightingale, night's comfort be!
Now let your voice most joyfully,
Most exquisitely soar;
Come, let your praise of God be heard,
For fast asleep is every bird
Save you, and sings no more;
Oh sing, sweet bird, and do not rest,
For you sing best
And best can raise
Your voice to God in sounds of praise.

Although the sun has gone away,
And in the darkness we must stay,
We still sing loud and strong
Of God's great goodness and His might,
Despite the darkness of the night,
And praise Him in our song.
Sing, then, sweet bird, before you rest,
For you sing best
And best can raise
Your voice to God in sounds of praise.

Now Echo, the unruly boy,
Takes part in our songs of joy;
He sings with us a while,
Tells us to banish weariness
To be, as he is, tireless
And slothful sleep beguile.
Sing on, sweet bird, you must not rest,
For you sing best,
And best can raise
Your voice to God in sounds of praise.

The silent stars up in the sky
Shine in praise of God on high,
And silently rejoice;
Poor, unmelodious bird, the owl,
Must sing *its* praise with hoot and howl,
It has no singing voice;
Sing sweetly, then, and do not rest,
For you sing best,
And best can raise
Your voice to God in sounds of praise.

Oh come, my dearest bird, to me!
Let us two not the dullest be,
And lie asleep all night long.
But let us, till the dawning day
Shall make these forests green and gay,
Pass time away in light song.
Sing, then, sweet bird, you must not rest,
For you sing best
And best can raise
Your voice to God in sounds of praise.'"

"Upon my soul," cried Schoolmaster Whackwell, "that was no wild beast, if it could sing such a song!"

And Tiraling replied: "But Father, you did not see it come creeping on all fours to the water, or slap the boar, or go barking up the tree! Of course, when it sang the lovely song so piously, when Echo made it resound in the trees upon which the moon shone as on a splendid church, when the dear nightingale joined in the singing, and the brook gurgled more merrily, and the forest listened more devoutly, and the clouds in the sky stopped racing by so fast, and the moon became brighter still . . . then all my fears were silenced. Before, my soul was turbulent like the sea when a great rock comes crashing in. But after the first verse, my soul was like a lake to which a fish that a vulture stole returns, sound and unharmed; and after the second verse, like a lake where a singing swan descends and leaves a shimmering wake; and after the third verse, like a lake on which a dove in flight lets drop a twig from the peaceful olive tree; and after the fourth verse, like a lake onto which a gentle wind blows a rose petal; and after the fifth verse, I felt like a tired little bee that wants to fly over the lake and cannot go on, and fears that it will fall into the water, and then falls on this rose petal . . . it was as if I were sailing safely and calmly on the little rose petal across the lake and landing on the other side in a flower-filled garden. My heart was as smooth as a mirror in which the moon gazes at itself, and my soul was at peace as I heard the lovely tiraling when the nightingale began to sing."

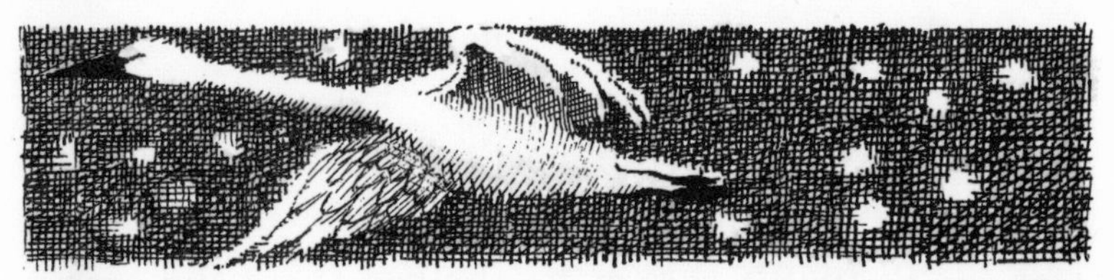

JUST THEN, Gripsgrabs interrupted. "Oh Tiraling," he said, "how you can talk! You look as shaggy as a bear, and yet your speech is sweet as honey! Why don't you simply say you were as frightened as I was the first time I stole something and began to learn gripsgrabs?"

"I did not feel as you did," Tiraling replied, "because I had done no wrong. Oh, dear brother Gripsgrabs, you have an evil trade! I hope you will soon be able to give it up."

"God grant it," said Grispsgrabs, growing very serious.

Now it was Piffpaff's turn to speak: "I can well imagine what a fright you had. Perhaps you felt as I did when... but listen: Once I pledged to shoot an apple from the hand of a sleeping child. The apple had cheeks as rosy as the child's, and the child held it pressed to its heart. Oh, how afraid I was! I trembled as I pulled the bow taut and *paff*, went the arrow, and there lay the child! I felt as if a mountain had fallen on me. But how was it with me a moment later? Why, the child stood before me, pulled me by the hair, and said: 'Now you must give me another apple! You spoiled the one I had!' Never was anyone happier or more relieved than I. The child gave me the apple with my arrow inside it. Look, I carry it in my quiver for eternal remembrance!" There were tears in Piffpaff's eyes as he showed them the arrow.

Tiraling embraced him and said: "Dear brother, I am so glad that you regret your rashness. But I did not feel as you did, because I took no such dreadful chance. Alas, your calling is a dangerous one, if you are prey to evil whims."

Piffpaff blushed and spoke: "I will never do such a thing again. That is why I carry this arrow in my quiver." And he put the arrow back with the others.

Then, all of a sudden, Tiraling jumped up from the bench. "I think I hear something now," he said, and ran outside.

"Poor fellow!" sighed Schoolmaster Whackwell. "One minute he speaks quite reasonably, and the next minute he acts as if he has lost his senses!"

Soon Tiraling came in again, muttering to himself: "There is still no word."

"Word of what?" they all wanted to know.

"I will tell you when the time comes," was all that he would say.

"NOW LET ME TELL you *my* story," said Pinkiepank. "I can well imagine how you felt, brother Piffpaff, when you shot that arrow. There was a time when I too thought that I had caused a great mischief. One day a little girl came to me in the pharmacy and said: 'Oh, dear Apothecary, won't you give me some good sweet pills for Mother, to make her well very soon? Because if she does not get well soon she cannot spin, and if she cannot spin there will be no yarn, and if there is no yarn my sisters and I cannot knit stockings, and if we don't knit stockings we cannot sell stockings, and if we can't sell stockings we'll get no money, and if we get no money we can't buy bread and will starve.'

"I looked in all the medicine jars for something good, and found what I thought was white sugar. I rolled some pills in it and gave them to the child. She licked a bit of the sugar off, and said: 'Oh, that is sweet, my mother will like that. And when she gets well, I will knit you a pair of stockings with a red flower design and a border of stars at the top.' Then she ran merrily out the door. When I went to arrange the medicine jars in their proper places . . . alas, what wretchedness befell me! For on the jar from which I thought I had taken sugar, was printed, in large letters: SUGAR OF LEAD. That is a deadly poison which looks just like sugar. In a frenzy, I dashed out of the pharmacy and ran through all the streets, looking for the child. I asked for her everywhere, but no one had seen her, and no one knew where she lived. I kept on running, right out the town gate, until I came to a little chapel all in ruins, where all sorts of wild herbs were growing. I wrung my hands in my despair, kneeled down before the crumbling altar and fervently prayed God to keep the poor mother and child alive.

"When I was done praying I felt calmer, and hope returned to my soul. I resolved to go back and ask the master apothecary if he knew of an antidote for the poison; perhaps I might yet find the child and her mother in time. But as I came to the pharmacy, despair took hold of me again, and I was tempted to take some of the poison myself. I opened the ill-fated jar and began to lick the white powder, when in came the master apothecary, holding a large licorice root in his hand. He grabbed me by the hair, beat me woefully with the licorice root, and shouted: 'Oh, you sweet-toothed sugar-licker! Now here's a licorice root for you! First you run around all day in the streets instead of helping me, and then you come back to steal the sugar!'

'Stop, master,' I cried. 'Don't kill me with your blows, for I have taken poison!'

'What poison, you idiot?' he asked.

'Isn't this sugar of lead,' said I, 'as the label says on the jar?'

'No,' he answered, laughing loudly. 'It's only sugar! I keep poisons behind lock and key, where careless people like you can't get at them. In all the jars you see here, there is nothing more harmful than plain white sugar!'

"Imagine my relief! I grabbed my master by his ears and kissed and embraced him a thousand times. Then, without stopping to say good-bye, I ran out of the pharmacy, out of the town and, as though some mysterious power were driving me on, back to the little chapel where I had prayed before. Once more I kneeled down and thanked God with all my might, until I dropped off to sleep in my exhaustion, still aching from my master's blows.

"When I got up the next morning, my back was swollen from the licorice thrashing. It pained me so, that I lay down again to rest a little longer. But no sooner did my back touch the ground than all the pain was gone! In amazement, I examined the spot where I had just lain, and found a beautiful little herb growing in great plenty there. Perhaps it had some magic healing power! It had certainly cured my back-ache . . . who knows, thought I, for what else it might be useful? I picked great bunches of it, and then I began my journey here, Father, because it was time to visit you.

"Before very long, I came to a forest and heard a child crying. I followed the sound and found the very same little girl I had been searching for! She was sitting under a tree, holding a small dog in her lap, and weeping bitterly. 'Poor child,' said I, 'did your mother die after all, that you are weeping so?'

'Oh no, dear Mr. Apothecary,' she answered. 'Mother is very well, thanks to your good pills. And the stockings I promised you are finished; I have been knitting night and day. Here they are . . . just look at the lovely red design!' I put them on and thanked her. Then I asked again why she was crying. 'I was on my way to bring you the stockings,' she said. 'I took our faithful little dog Dauntless too, because he was sick and I thought you might have some pills for him. But just think! When I came to this place, poor little Dauntless was so tired he could not go on. I sat down with him. He looked at me sadly, wagged his tail a bit, stretched himself and now he lies in my lap, so still. Oh, if only you had come sooner, perhaps you could have helped him . . . but now, surely, it is too late!'

'Let me see what can be done,' I said. I took some of my herbs, pressed their juice into the dog's mouth, then he opened his eyes; a little more juice, and he wagged his tail the tiniest little bit; still more juice, and he licked my hands and jumped up joyfully on the child, who thanked me over and over again. Now that he was well again, little Dauntless did all his tricks for me: fetch, hide and seek, pay attention, beg, stand guard, leap over the stick, what does the dog say, and dance. For his last trick, he played dead, after which he got up and licked my hands in thanks for my making him well. Then we parted, the little girl, her dog, and I, and I continued my way here. Look . . . I am still wearing the fine stockings, and see, here is my wonderful herb Arise!"

WHILE THE OTHERS were admiring Pinkiepank's stockings and herbs, Tiraling ran outside again, as suddenly as before, to see if the messenger had arrived. He soon returned, looking downcast, because there was still no news.

Splishsplosh was next to tell his story. "Since we are comparing moments of fright," he said, "let me tell you of a great fright I once had: One day I went out fishing in a very small rowboat. There were no other fishermen out that day except one, whom I knew for a cruel, harsh man. His boat was quite close to mine. I cast my net, and caught a great big fish that fought and flailed its tail. I struck it with my oar and slit its belly open. Imagine my amazement when I found a beautiful gold ring inside! Happily I put it on my finger. Then, just as I was going to cast my net again, a great wave surged up between my boat and the other fisherman's. From out of its foam arose a mermaid! You should have seen her lovely, long green hair, the little gold crown with pearls she wore, and the shells and corals around her neck. She held out her hands to the cruel fisherman, crying out most piteously. But instead of helping, he threw a small harpoon at the poor little mermaid and hit her in the side. With a heart-rending cry, she tried to dive down to the bottom of the sea. But she could not, because she was wounded, and so she turned toward my boat. I rowed toward her as fast as I could, and when she stretched her arms out to me, I could see the red blood trickling from her side.

'For the sake of almighty God,' she cried, 'in Whose eyes you are my brother, save my young life!' All the while, the cruel fisherman pursued her. As I pulled her up into my boat, his boat was so close to mine that he could touch me with his oar.

'Splishsplosh,' he roared, 'give me your mermaid, or I will strike you dead!'

'I cannot give her to you,' I replied, 'for she has asked my help in God's name.'

He struck me then; I struck him back, and while we were battling, a storm drove our two boats out to sea. I offered to give him all my fish if he would let

me keep the mermaid, but he demanded my net, too, and even my boat. 'Not that!' I said. But the mermaid implored me, so I gave in. The wind had forced us onto a sand shoal, and there the cruel man knocked me out of my boat, hurling the poor mermaid after me. 'Don't leave me stranded on this shoal in the middle of the sea!' I begged.

'Then give me the ring that glitters on your finger,' he demanded.

I was just about to yield it up, when the mermaid cried out: "My ring, my ring! For Heaven's sake, don't give him my ring!' And she snatched the ring from me. At this, the evil fisherman tried to strike her; but I parried his blow, and again we fought. Since he was the stronger, he threw me to the ground. As I lay there, I heard the mermaid calling with a voice as sharp as the nose of a swordfish:

> 'Korali, Korali, woe is me,
> Margaris dies on the wide, wide, sea!'

"Then a wave rose mountain-high. It hurled the evil fisherman out into the billows, and swept both boats away. I sat there with the wounded mermaid, all alone on the sand shoal . . . no help in sight, and night was upon us. 'Miserable mermaid!' I said, 'what misfortune you have brought me! For your sake I must perish here, and you are not even a human being! I shudder when I look at you and see your scaly fish's tail!'

'Poor Splishsplosh,' she answered, 'don't regret that you were kind, but pull the harpoon from my side and bandage up my wound!' I did what she asked, and while I was tending her wound, she sang in an enchanting voice:

'With tender care you staunch my blood,
To you the sea will not be rude;
Its mildest and its wildest flood
Will guard you as your mother would.
You will dive, and swim, and float,
Needing neither oar nor boat;
The storm will carry you aloft,
Its fiercest waves turn meek and mild
To cradle you, as sweet and soft
As any mother would her child.
Because you have been kind to me,
You will fare well upon the sea.'

"When her song was finished, she pulled me gently down with her through the waves. What she had promised came true . . . I could breathe as freely in the water as on dry land! She pulled me down, down, all the way to the bottom of the sea. There she knocked at a shimmering, pearly door and called:

'Open the door, open it wide,
Dear Korali, for your own bride.'

"Korali replied from inside:

'I will not open up this door
Till Margaris has my ring once more.'

MARGARIS:

'I bring the ring, the fisherman, too,
Who found it in a fish, to you.'

KORALI:

'With stones I'll beat the bad man dead
And hang him in the corals red.'

MARGARIS:

'No! No! He gave his net and oar
So that I might be free once more.'

KORALI:

'Then he shall have such net and oar
As no one ever had before.'

MARGARIS:

'Even his boat this good man gave,
Margaris' sweet life to save.'

KORALI:

'Then will I build him, with my own hand,
A boat that will take him o'er cliffs and sand.'

MARGARIS:

'While on the sandy shoal maroon'd,
That good man bandaged up my wound.'

KORALI:

'May he breathe the salt sea as though it were
As sweet and fresh as heaven's air.'

"Then Korali, who was a merman, opened the door and embraced his bride. He thanked me with all his heart for saving her, and gave me all the things he had promised. The first gift was an oar made of fish scales, tortoise shell and mother-of-pearl. 'This oar,' he said, 'will never tire you. The more you row with it, the greater will your strength be.' The second gift was a net made of green mermaid's hair, into which, he promised, the fish would flock with greatest joy. Then he built me a boat of rushes with fins like a fish, so light that it glides over the water like a swallow in flight. And the last gift—breathing under water as freely as on earth—had already been granted me when I staunched the mermaid's blood.

"When it was time to leave them, Korali filled my new boat with the finest shells, pearls and corals. Then the merman and the mermaid pulled my boat . . . softly, softly . . . up to the surface of the sea. I bade them a fond farewell, and watched them vanish into the waves. In no time at all my wonderful little boat reached the land. I hid it and its precious cargo in a lonely inlet where no one can find it, and hurried here to our reunion."

WHEN SPLISHSPLOSH had finished, Schoolmaster Whackwell turned to Tiraling and said: "You must go on with *your* story now. We still don't know what sort of creature it was that sang the song to the nightingale!" And Tiraling continued:

"I so enjoyed the lovely song and the nightingale joining in, and the Echo, that when it was over I got up to ask the singer to begin again. But scarcely had I made a sound than it started barking again and, worse still, threw some thick twigs down at me from the tree. One of them hit me so hard on the nose that I cried out: 'Dear God, my nose, my nose!'

"This brought the creature down from the tree, lightning-quick. Before I knew what was happening, it grabbed hold of me and exclaimed: 'Oh, I beg a thousand pardons,' and tapped me on the nose with such hard, bony fingers, that the pain was greater than before.

" 'Pray tell,' said I, 'who *are* you, that you can whistle like a bird, bark like a dog, climb trees like a wildcat, go on all fours to the stream to drink, and then sing such melodious songs? Could it be you are a proper Christian, and not a wild beast after all?'

" 'I am the Crabapple Hermit,' he replied. 'I have lived in this forest for eighty years. You see, I keep a school for birds here and teach them to sing correctly.

I speak their languages, as well as the languages of other beasts. And living among them as I do, I want them to think well of me, so I assume their ways. Do forgive me . . . in all my long years here, I have not seen another human being. I took you for a wildcat climbing up the tree, and thought you might want to eat up my students, the birds. That is why I barked like a dog, to frighten you away!'

"Then I told him that I was called Tiraling, that tiraling was my calling, and that I had followed my calling into the wild wood so I might learn the languages of birds.

" 'Good', he said, 'very good! You have come to the right place, for I will gladly teach you all I know.'

"When it was daylight, I saw what the hermit looked like: An old, old monkey, covered from head to toe with white hair from his head and beard. No wonder I had mistaken him for a wild animal! Soon the birds awoke, and he led them in a lovely morning song. Then he took leave of them. 'They will have their vacation now,' he told me. 'You see, they must build nests, lay eggs, and hatch their young. Meanwhile, I will instruct you in their ABC.'

"I spent a long time with the hermit, trying to learn all he could teach me. I was not kept from my studies by too much food or drink, because we ate only roots, herbs and bird-food—gnats, spiders, little bugs, ant eggs, juniper berries and the like. The hermit always

told me to eat the favorite food of the bird whose language I was just learning. One day, while studying the fieldfare's language, I sat in a juniper bush and ate berries, for those are the fieldfare's special delight. As I was sitting there, I suddenly heard a human voice close by, saying: 'Alas, I should not have left my royal father's side! Now I am lost in this wild wood, and cannot find King Pompam'."

"Then I heard a second, most peculiar, voice. It was saying the oddest things that made no sense at all: 'Most humble Princess Ringlejing, I am your disrespectful servant! Oh, where is the snow-black raven who stole the cowbell from your pitch-white neck? I followed bird and bell-sound, as you commanded me, but now I see no bird and hear no bell. And though I have the title of Travel Minister, the only way I know is to the kitchen, to the wine cellar, and to bed. There are no kitchens and no wine cellars and no beds in this silly wilderness, and I don't know where to go!'

" 'You are a foolish fool,' the first voice scolded. When will you learn to call me most *noble*, not most humble, princess, and say you are my *respectful* servant, as you ought to be? For shame, how can a raven be black as snow, or my neck be white as pitch? And dare you call my dainty silver bell a cow-bell?'

"This voice belonged to the most beautiful princess in all the world. I saw her then, as she stepped out into a clearing. She wore a glittering gold crown on her green hat, a gray traveling gown embroidered all over with gold, and a pair of red morocco boots with golden spurs. The second voice belonged to her companion, who was as comical as she was fair. His jacket and trousers were of all imaginable colors, his white hat was shaped like a funnel, and with his wooden sword in hand he looked as foolish as can be. I laughed at him, but only for a moment. Longer than that I could not bear to look away from the most beautiful Princess Ringlejing.

"The princess looked down and saw bluebells growing where she stood. 'Oh, look at the lovely flowers,' she cried out, 'the lovely, silent little bells! I'll stay and make a wreath of them. You go, my dear fool, and find someone who will show us the way back to the road.'

" 'Sweet Princess Ringlejing,' said the fool, 'what if a bear should come and take you for a honeycomb?'

" 'Do as I tell you,' she commanded, 'and don't disturb my meditations!'

"To which he replied: 'I am not a disturber, I am the Minister of Travel! I would be happy to obey your command, only I don't know where I should go!'

" 'Go to that big oak tree,' said Princess Ringlejing. 'I see some footprints over there. Perhaps you will find someone who can show us the way.'

"The fool was still delaying. 'Princess,' he said, 'if you know how to mend shoes, then we are saved.'

" 'Whatever do you mean?' asked Ringlejing.

"And he answered: 'Why, then we can stay here and be cobblers, and mend the wild beasts' shoes. For I could swear those are a bear's footprints, and not the footprints of a man.'

" 'Don't swear,' said Ringlejing, 'just go and do what I tell you.' So the fool followed the footprints, while the princess made herself a wreath of bluebells, and sang this lovely song:

'Silver bells ring merrily
Playing with a breath of air,
Ring, ring, ringlejing.
But a sweeter sight to see
Are the little bluebells there,
When silently they ring in spring.

Raven, raven, I don't care
Where you take my silver bell,
Ring, ring, ringlejing.
From now on I want to wear
Bluebells that look just as well
And in peaceful silence ring.

My silver bell rang crystal-clear,
No matter where I walked or stood,
Ring, ring, ringlejing.
Now no human ear can hear
When I go skipping through the wood,
Little bluebells do not ring.

Everybody looked at me,
Wherever I would walk along,
Ring, ring, ringlejing.
Now I can hide so quietly
And see the birds, and hear their song.
These new bluebells will not ring.

Oh, how cold the world was then,
When I always had to hear
Ring, ring, ringlejing.
Now the birds can sing again
And I, be happy. Bluebells, dear,
I am so glad you do not ring!'

"The princess had such a sweet voice that all the birds were still and listened, the stream murmured more softly and listened, and the bluebells bent willingly toward her in order to be plucked.

"Meanwhile, the fool had gone to the old oak tree, as the princess had commanded. The tree was hollow; inside it sat the Crabapple Hermit, all crouched and bent. All that could be seen of him was his long nose peeking out and his white beard flowing down like a waterfall. This made the fool cry out in fright and turn six somersaults back to the princess. 'Oh dear,' he said, 'that oak tree has eaten up a billygoat. The goat's beard is still hanging from its mouth! What if the tree will eat us up, too?'

"The princess looked at the oak tree and said: 'Oh, you cowardly fool! I can see by the long nose that there is a human being in there. Go back and ask him who he is.' So the fool went back to the tree and spoke:

'Big nose, big beard, to both I bring
Respects from Princess Ringlejing,
Who ordered me to ask of you,
Are you proper folk, you two?'

"Then the hermit mumbled with a dusky voice:

'I am an old, old anchorite.'

"The fool laughed and, also mumbling and making his voice very dusky, said to Ringlejing:

'He says he makes gold anchors bright."

"Ringlejing smiled and said:

'Go and ask him once again
Who, in this wild forest glen
Far from the sea, who in his right
Senses needs gold anchors bright?'

"The fool went back and spoke:

'Big nose, big beard, to you I bring
A smile from Princess Ringlejing.
She says that no one in his right
Senses here needs anchors bright.'

"Again the hermit mumbled:

'I said I'm an old anchorite.'

"And the fool told Ringlejing:

'He's a cold banker, if I heard him right.'

"Ringlejing smiled again and said:

'Go and ask him once again
Who, in this wild forest glen,
Would be a banker, warm or cold?
There's no need for silver here, no need for gold!'

"So the fool went back and asked:

'Big nose, big beard, again I bring
A smile from Princess Ringlejing.
She doubts that there are bankers here,
And thinks that story's very queer.'

"The hermit mumbled:

'I live in pious solitude.'

"And the fool said to Ringlejing:

'He says, why he's a soldier rude.'

"Then Ringlejing said:

'Go and ask him once again
What, in this wild forest glen,
A soldier rude or ev'n polite
Might find to do by day or night?'

"So the fool asked again, and the hermit replied:

'I tell you, I'm a hermit!'

"The fool spoke:

'He says he has a firm wit!'

"And the princess said:

'We do not doubt his sanity,
We merely ask who he might be!'

"The fool asked again, and the hermit said:

'I live here in seclusion!'

"The fool told the princess:

'He says life's an illusion.'

"And the princess said:

'Let him philosophize in quiet!
Try asking, what's his diet?'

"So the fool asked the hermit what he ate, and the hermit replied, still mumbling:

'I eat leaves and grasses.'

"And the fool said:

'He eats lads and lasses.'

"Impatient, the hermit said again:

'I eat leaves and grasses,
Roots and small plants,
Mushrooms and berries,
Bugs, crickets and insects.'

"And the fool rattled off after him:

'He eats lads and lasses,
Boots and tall aunts,
Rush brooms and bears,
Rugs, tickets, and inspectors.'

"This was too much! We all came rushing out—the hermit from his hollow oak, Ringlejing from among her bluebells, and I from my juniper bush—ready to thrash the fool for twisting the words so foolishly. But before we could lay hands on him, he leaped over the stream like a hare, and ran off into the wood. Now the Crabapple Hermit introduced himself to the princess without any more mumbling, and introduced me as his student. 'But who are you?' he asked. 'And what are you doing in this wild wood?'

"'I am Princess Ringlejing,' she answered, 'daughter of Pompam, the King of Dingdongdom. We came traveling this way in search of the great golden clapper from our castle bell. You see, it disappeared the other day while we were having a bell-ringing contest in our country. Someone must have stolen it and taken it away. As we were walking, not far from here, I left my father's side for a moment and lingered behind with the fool. Just then I slipped, and lost the little jinglebell that all the crown princesses of Dingdongdom have always worn. I could not find it anywhere; neither could my fool. But a raven saw it hanging from a twig and carried it off in his beak.

We followed its ringing as far as we could, and now we are lost in this wild wood, and cannot hear it any more. Dear hermit, please speak to the birds for me. Perhaps they have seen the raven with my bell, or, better still, can tell me where my father is!'

"The hermit and I called the birds together. We coaxed them to come in every bird language we knew, and they came flying along from all directions. None of them had anything to tell us, except another raven. 'I know all about it,' he boasted. 'My fellow raven is taking Ringlejing's bell to Snorrasper, the giant. Snorrasper, in case you do not know, is king of all night watchmen. He lives on a high rock in the middle of the sea. Let the princess follow me! I will guide her to the rock. She will find the golden clapper there, and her father Pompam, too.'

"Was this raven to be trusted? I did not like his piercing eyes, or his croaking, boastful voice. But the princess decided to follow him . . . what else could she do? I prayed with the Crabapple Hermit that all would be well. Then Ringlejing called her fool, and he came running back from across the stream. His pockets bulged with hazelnuts, his hands and mouth were stained from the blueberries he had been eating. The hermit gave Ringlejing a fresh honeycomb to take along on her journey; I picked the most beautiful bluebells for her and planted them by their roots in

the fool's funnel-shaped hat. In return she gave the hermit a kiss, and to me she gave a miniature portrait of herself studded with diamonds. I was kissing the hem of her gown when the raven croaked: 'March! March! We must not delay, we must go a long way!' She gave us her hand in farewell, and we wept bitterly because she was leaving.

"When the time came to return to you, dear Father, I, too, took leave of the Crabapple Hermit, embracing him many times and thanking him for all he had taught me. I said good-bye to all the birds, and begged them to come to me here if they had news of the princess. But wait . . . just now I think I really do hear something outside!"

The others heard it too. It was the melodious but loud and insistent call of a bird, and it came from the tree in the garden. Once again, Tiraling jumped up and went outside. This time he stayed there quite a while.

He returned looking excited, but also troubled. "At last there is news of Princess Ringlejing," he said. "It was a thrush who brought it. Oh, that I had never trusted the raven and let the princess follow him! That wicked bird is in Snorrasper's employ, and so is the raven who stole her silver bell. It was Snorrasper himself who stole Dingdongdom's golden clapper, and now he has Dingdongdom's princess, too. The raven led the princess and the fool to the shore. Snorrasper lay in wait for them there, and carried them off to his rock in the middle of the sea. Alas, they did not find King Pompam there; it was a lie that he went to Snorrasper's rock, for Ringlejing's father has long since gone home. Poor Ringlejing! The dreadful king of night watchmen holds her captive, and she must sit all day on that high rock, holding his head in her lap, and must sing to him so he can sleep. For Snorrasper sleeps by day and rules the night watchmen by night. And the poor fool must beat a whip over the water all day long, to keep the frogs from croaking and disturbing the giant's sleep. But back in Dingdongdom, King Pompam has proclaimed that whoever frees his daughter and finds the golden clapper from the castle bell shall have Ringlejing to wife and get half of the kingdom, too. This is what the thrush told me. I know you will all help me rescue Ringlejing. Let us go . . . there is no time to lose!"

TIRALING showed the portrait of the princess to his father and his brothers. They all admired her beauty and agreed to find her right away. The schoolmaster put on his black coat, took up his cane, and closed the door.

"I will save her from Snorrasper," Gripsgrabs promised. "With the help of my two daggers, I will climb the rock as nimbly as a cat."

Splishsplosh said: "My boat will take us there more swiftly than a swallow."

Piffpaff said: "I will shoot an arrow and kill Snorrasper, if need be."

Pinkiepank said: "I will stand by with my herb Arise, in case someone should meet with misfortune."

And Whackwell said: "I will be master in all the schools when half the kingdom of Dingdongdom is ours!"

After several days' journeying, they came to the sea. Splishsplosh found his wonderful boat where he had hidden it, with all its treasures safe inside. "These pearls, shells and corals I will give to the princess for a wedding gift," he said. They all got into the boat and Splishsplosh rowed. With every oar stroke, the boat sped another mile out to sea.

Soon they came to the tall, steep rock out in the middle of the sea. There, at the foot of it, stood the poor fool, beating a whip over the water to keep the frogs quiet. When he caught sight of Tiraling, he gave a thousand signs of joy, but motioned that everybody should keep very still.

Splishsplosh rowed the boat right up to the rock. Gripsgrabs prepared to scale it, and all the brothers held their breath to see how he would do it. It was an awesome sight: First he rolled up his sleeves and took a dagger into each hand. Then he thrust the dagger at his right into a rock cleft and swung himself up; next he thrust the dagger at his left higher into the rock and again swung himself up, at the same time pulling the first dagger out of its cleft and sinking it into another, still higher. Again he swung

himself up, and so on, all the way to the top. Down in the boat, his father and brothers were afraid for him, and prayed that God might help him.

A terrible danger beset him midway between the bottom and the top. He was holding on to the dagger at his left and was about to thrust the right dagger higher, when a raven came flying at him with menacing caw-caw and a great flapping of wings. It was the very same one who had stolen Ringlejing's bell! In terror, Gripsgrabs let the dagger fall from his right hand into the sea. There he was, holding on for dear life to the dagger at his left, fending the raven off with his right hand, and unable to move either forward or back!

Within a split second, Splishsplosh plunged from the boat to the bottom of the sea to retrieve the fallen dagger, while Piffpaff grabbed an arrow and shot the raven, who dropped, wounded, into the boat. In a trice, Splishsplosh came out of the sea with the dagger. Piffpaff took it and shot it, as if it were an arrow, back up to Gripsgrabs, who caught it in his right hand and continued his way up to the top.

Now that all was well again with Gripsgrabs, Tiraling went to speak to the wounded raven. The raven moaned and said in raven language: "I deserve to die for stealing Princess Ringlejing's bell!"

"Return it," said Tiraling, "and you need not die."

"It is yours," said the raven. Tiraling broke the string by which it hung from the raven's neck, and kept the bell for Ringlejing. Then Pinkiepank squeezed a little juice from the herb Arise into the raven's wound, and he was well again, and flew away.

Meanwhile Gripsgrabs had reached the top of the rock. There stood a giant guardhouse from which came Snorrasper's frightful snoring, and Princess Ringlejing's soft song:

"Snorrasper, snore and rasp,
God free me from your grasp!
Or I must stay till I am dead.
He gives me only crusts of bread,
And I must sing, and hold his head
From dawn until he sees the red
Glow of dusk, and leaves his bed.
His giant form fills me with dread,
I pray I might be rescued.

Snorrasper, snore and rasp,
God free me from your grasp!
His monstrous head is in my lap,
My arm is fastened with a strap
To his braid... I watch him nap,
His snoring mouth is a dark gap,
I dare not move, or he will slap
My face. Oh, what a wretched trap!

Snorrasper, snore and rasp,
God free me from your grasp!
More wretchedness begins at night,
When he gets up and out of spite
Pinches me with all his might!
Then I must make a giant white
Flour dumpling, make it right
Away for his huge appetite.

Snorrasper, snore and rasp,
God free me from your grasp!
When he has eaten this great mound
Of food, he moves, with leap and bound,
He twirls his halbert round and round,
And blows his horn. The mighty sound
Makes this rock shake from top to ground...
Oh, that my rescuer were found!

Snorrasper, snore and rasp,
God free me from your grasp!
When his horn blasts out its call,
I hear the turmoil and the brawl
Of his night watchmen come from all
Lands on earth, both great and small;
Their noise, from tower or from wall,
Resounds here, in their ruler's hall.

Snorrasper, snore and rasp,
God free me from your grasp!
Oh starry night, so dear to me
In that sweet time when I was free,
When moonlight tinted every tree,
When sleep built castles fair to see,
When fleetest dreams came silently,
Here must you wild and noisy be!

Snorrasper, snore and rasp,
God free me from your grasp!
No flute, no lute, no harp sounds clear,
No jinglebells that I held dear
In days gone by can help me here.
All alone and without cheer
I lull the giant whom I fear
And wish deliverance were near.

Snorrasper, snore and rasp,
God free me from your grasp!
My father Pompam's far away,
Nothing but the sea's salt spray
For miles and miles I see, and pray
That God will pity my dismay
And send to me without delay
A rescuer . . . this very day!"

While she was singing, Gripsgrabs thought of a way to save her. What he needed if his plan was to succeed were some flies or bees, to put near Snorrasper's ears. But were there any insects so far away from land? He looked around and—yes, he caught a few tired flies and even a bumblebee, who had ventured out over the sea to this rock. Holding them imprisoned in his hand, he opened the door to the guardhouse quietly . . . quietly. Ringlejing trembled with joy at the sight of her rescuer. "Just keep on singing," he whispered, "and I will have you off this rock in no time at all!" Then, with a shudder, Gripsgrabs looked at the giant Snorrasper lying there snoring, his head in Ringlejing's lap. Every time he snored and rasped, he made the dust and sand from down below come flying up in the air. From his head hung a long, black braid which was securely tied to poor Ringlejing's arm, and on his back was a pair of wings like those of an enormous bat. His night watchman's horn hung on the wall; it was so large that a man could easily sleep inside. Next to it hung his watchman's bag, which was as big as a door, and in a corner stood his halbert, a very dangerous-looking weapon indeed.

Gripsgrabs stopped up the horn, ripped up the bag, and hid the halbert. Then he stuck the buzzing flies and the bumblebee into the wisps of hair which covered the giant's ears, so that Snorrasper would hear them buzz and hum there, and think Ringlejing was still singing. Ringlejing could stop now. Gripsgrabs freed her arm from Snorrasper's braid. Next, he took the rusty old cauldron in which Ringlejing cooked the giant's dumplings every night . . . softly, softly, the princess got up, and Gripsgrabs pushed the cauldron under Snorrasper's head for a pillow. All the while, the giant went on snoring, quite as if he were still lying in Ringlejing's lap. There was only one other thing left to do . . . find the golden clapper from Dingdongdom's castle bell. And there it stood, against the wall, right behind Snorrasper! Gripsgrabs grabbed it,

and hurled it down to the bottom of the rock where his brothers could take it and lift it safely into the boat. But how was he to get the princess down the rock? He could not carry her with him, because he needed both his hands to grip the daggers. Luckily, the princess was small enough to fit into the pail Snorrasper used to send food down to the fool. Gripsgrabs lifted her in and gently lowered her by the pulley rope. Then he climbed down himself.

Speechless with joy at finding her again, Tiraling helped the princess out of the bucket and into the boat. The fool got in too, and Gripsgrabs also, after his dangerous descent. Without a moment's delay, Splishsplosh plunged his oar into the water so forcefully that the boat darted away like an arrow over the sea.

They had not gone very far when Snorrasper awoke from his sleep. The flies and bumblebee had crept out of his hair; the flies flew away, but the bumblebee sat itself down on his red nose. When the buzzing and humming stopped, Snorrasper thought Ringlejing had stopped singing, and, still half asleep, he said: "Ringlejing, Ringlejing, sing some more sweet songs to me, or I will hit you cruelly." But since there was still no singing, and since at that moment the bumblebee stung him sharply on the nose, Snorrasper grew furious and struck out with his fists. Instead of striking Ringlejing, his fists struck the rusty cauldron, and he cried, "Ouch, ouch!" Up he jumped, and ran around on the rock, but Ringlejing was nowhere to be found. Then he saw the little boat floating away out on the wide, wide sea. "So there you are," he roared, groping for his halbert. He did not find that either, because Gripsgrabs had hidden it. "Well, then," he said, "I'll sound my horn to assemble all night watchmen!" But the horn was stopped up, and though he nearly blew his cheeks asunder, it did not make a sound.

"Just wait, you wretched Ringlejing!" he shouted. "I'll get you yet, and your rescuer, too." With that, he spread his bats' wings and flew—flutter, flutter—over the sea after the boat.

"Heaven help us, here comes Snorrasper!" cried Ringlejing, and she lay down flat so that the giant should not see her. But Snorrasper came flying nearer like a swift, black cloud. Splishsplosh made the boat move even faster than before, but it was in vain; Snorrasper came closer and closer. Just as he was poised above them, ready to descend, *piffpaff* went Piffpaff's arrow, and shot the giant right through his heart. He came hurtling down, stone dead, into the water, and one of his wide bats' wings struck the boat such a mighty blow that it swept them all together, helter-skelter, into the stern.

Pompam embraced his daughter, and the schoolmaster, and all the brothers, too. "Now tell me," he said, "which one of you should have my daughter and half my kingdom? I promised that whoever would bring the princess back should have her to wife, but all *six* of you have brought her!"

Then Gripsgrabs said: "I freed her from Snorrasper."

And Piffpaff: "I shot an arrow through Snorrasper's heart."

And Splishsplosh: "I rowed her to shore in my boat."

And Pinkiepank: "I cured her with my magic herb."

And Whackwell: "I am the father of all of you, so she is rightly mine."

Only Tiraling said not a word. If it had not been for him, the princess would not have been rescued at all; but he was never one to brag. He looked so woebegone, though, to think Ringlejing might not be his after all, that his father and brothers had pity on him and said: "Never mind, Tiraling, we know you love her with all your heart!" Then Ringlejing threw her arms around his neck and kissed him, so that King Pompam could have no more doubt who her husband was to be. Tiraling gave her back her silver bell which the raven had stolen and then returned to him. But Ringlejing did not want it. She said she would rather have the simple, silent bluebells that grew in the woods where they would make their home.

"Very well," said Pompam. "Now let us divide the kingdom." He took a map, and drew a line through the middle. Tiraling chose his half, and then divided it equally among his father and brothers. For himself he kept nothing, because all he wanted was to live in the woods with Ringlejing, peacefully and happily, among their friends the birds.

Piffpaff, in his fifth of the kingdom, built a great shooting range for marksmen; Splishsplosh stocked all his lakes and ponds with fish; Pinkiepank started a vast herb garden; Gripsgrabs blazed trails on all his mountains, but gave up the thieving part of his art; Schoolmaster Whackwell built a great school in his fifth of the kingdom, and also became headmaster of all the schools in the land.

When the wedding day came, Ringlejing gave away, to the children of Dingdongdom, all the corals, pearls and seashells that Splishsplosh had given her. On that day, once again, all the bells of the kingdom rang, and the big castle bell rang out this whole amazing tale for everyone to hear. I was there, and I heard it, too.